Because a Little Bug went Ka- CHOO!

By
Rosetta Stone

Illustrated by
Michael Frith

COLLINS

Beginner Books

Trademark of Random House Inc.
Authorised user HarperCollins*Publishers* Ltd

4 6 8 10 9 7 5

ISBN 0 00 171320 5 (paperback)
ISBN 0 00 171163 6 (hardback)

A Beginner Book published by arrangement with
Random House Inc., New York, USA
First published in the UK 1976

Printed and bound in Hong Kong

You may not believe it,
but here's how it happened.

One fine summer morning . . .

. . . a little bug sneezed.

Because of that sneeze,
a little seed dropped.

Because that seed dropped,
a worm got hit.

Because he got hit,
that worm got mad.

Because he got mad,
he kicked a tree.

Because of that kick,
a coconut dropped.

Because
that nut
dropped,
a turtle
got bopped.

Because he got bopped,
that turtle named Jake
fell on his back
with a splash
in the lake.

Because of that splash,
a hen got wet.

Because she got wet,
that hen got mad.

Because she got mad,
that hen kicked a bucket.

Because of that kick,
the bucket went up.

Because it went up . . .

. . . the bucket
came down.

Because it came down,
it hit Farmer Brown.

And
that
bucket
got
stuck
on
his
head.

Because it got stuck,
Farmer Brown
phoned for help.

Because of his phone call,
policemen came speeding.

Because they were speeding,
they hit a big stone.

And so one policeman
flew up all alone.

Because he flew up . . .

. . . he
had
to
come
down.

And because he came down
on the boat Mary Lou . . .
and because he hit hard . . .

he went right on through.

He made a big hole
in the boat Mary Lou.

Because of that hole,
the boat started to sink.
And because it was sinking . . .
well, what do you think?

Everyone, EVERYONE started to yelp.

And Mrs. Brown called
on the phone for more help.

Because of her phone call,
MORE help came . . . FAST!

They tied a strong rope
to the Mary Lou's mast.

And because of that rope
the boat didn't go down.
But it had to be fixed.
So they started for town.

And because
they went THERE—
it's true, I'm afraid—
they ran right into
a circus parade.

And THAT started something
they'll never forget.

And as far as I know
it is going on yet.

And that's how it happened.

Believe me. It's true.

Because . . .

just because . . .

a small bug

went KA-CHOO!

Learning to read is fun with Beginner Books

I CAN READ IT ALL BY MYSELF

Beginner Books

FIRST get started with:

Ten Apples Up On Top
Dr. Seuss

Go Dog Go
P D Eastman

Put Me in the Zoo
Robert LopShire

THEN gain confidence with:

Dr. Seuss's ABC*
Dr. Seuss

Fox in Sox*
Dr. Seuss

Green Eggs and Ham*
Dr. Seuss

Hop on Pop*
Dr. Seuss

I Can Read With My Eyes Shut
Dr. Seuss

I Wish That I Had Duck Feet
Dr. Seuss

One Fish, Two Fish*
Dr. Seuss

Oh, the Thinks You Can Think!
Dr. Seuss

Please Try to Remember the First of Octember
Dr. Seuss

Wacky Wednesday
Dr. Seuss

Are You My Mother?
P D Eastman

Because a Little Bug Went Ka-choo!
Rosetta Stone

Best Nest
P D Eastman

Come Over to My House
Theo. LeSieg

The Digging-est Dog
Al Perkins

I Am Not Going to Get Up Today!
Theo. LeSieg

It's Not Easy Being a Bunny!
Marilyn Sadler

I Want to Be Somebody New
Robert LopShire

Maybe You Should Fly a Jet!
Theo. LeSieg

Robert the Rose Horse
Joan Heilbroner

The Very Bad Bunny
Joan Heilbroner

THEN take off with:

The Cat in the Hat*
Dr. Seuss

The Cat in the Hat Comes Back*
Dr. Seuss

Oh Say Can You Say?
Dr. Seuss

My Book About Me
Dr. Seuss

A Big Ball of String
Marion Holland

Chitty Chitty Bang Bang!
Ian Fleming

A Fish Out of Water
Helen Palmer

A Fly Went By
Mike McClintock

The King, the Mice and the Cheese
N & E Gurney

Sam and the Firefly
P D Eastman

BERENSTAIN BEAR BOOKS
By Stan & Jan Berenstain

The Bear Detectives

The Bear Scouts

The Bears' Christmas

The Bears' Holiday

The Bears' Picnic

The Berenstain Bears and the Missing Dinosaur Bones

The Big Honey Hunt

The Bike Lesson

THEN you won't quite be ready to go to college. But you'll be well on your way!

From the Dr. Seuss Classic Collection